# Alexandra

## Siobhán Parkinson

Illustrated by
### Carol Betera

Little Island

*For Orla and Olivia (with a kiss inside)*

ALEXANDRA
Published 2014
by Little Island
7 Kenilworth Park
Dublin 6W
Ireland

www.littleisland.ie

ISBN 978-1-908195-87-6

British Library Cataloguing Data. A CIP catalogue record for this book is available
from the British Library.

Design by Fidelma Slattery @ Someday.ie

Printed in Spain by Graficas Castuera

Little Island receives financial assistance from
The Arts Council (An Chomhairle Ealaíon), Dublin, Ireland.

10 9 8 7 6 5 4 3 2 1

Alexandra
Changes
her
Name

Alexandra didn't like being called Alexandra.

'It's too long,' she said to her mum. 'Al-ex-and-ra. My friends can't say it properly.'

'Well then,' said her mum, 'we'll have to shorten it. Would you like to be called Alex?'

'Hmm,' said Alexandra. 'Alex. I don't know.'

'Or Sandra?' suggested her mum.

'Hmm,' said Alexandra. 'Sandra. I don't know.'

'Well, you don't need to decide right now,' her mum said. 'You can sleep on it. Good night, Alexandra.'

The next morning Alexandra said to her mum, 'Today, I think I will be Alex.'

'That's fine, Alex,' said her mum. 'Now, what would you like to wear?'

'My Alex clothes,' said Alexandra. 'That's my bright red boots and my big floppy sunhat.'

'Your bright red boots and your big floppy sunhat,' said her mum. 'There you go.'

Alexandra spent the day kicking in puddles – *sploosh*! – with her bright red boots, and she waved her big floppy sunhat – *whoooeeee*! – at all the people going by in their cars.

The next morning her mum said, 'Good morning, Alex.'

'No,' said Alexandra. 'Today I think I will be Sandra.'

'That's fine, Sandra,' said her mum. 'And what would you like to wear today?'

'Today I will wear my Sandra clothes. That's my sparkly sandals and my best hair ribbon.'

'OK,' said Alexandra's mum. 'Your sparkly sandals and your best hair ribbon it is.'

Alexandra spent the day playing tea-parties under the cherry tree in the garden – *chink, chink* – and she twinkled her fingers – *toodle-oo-oo!* – at all the people going by in their cars.

The next morning her mum said, 'Good morning, Sandra.'

'No,' said Alexandra. 'Today I am going to be Alexandra again.'

'Why's that?' asked her mum. 'Have you got tired of your bright red boots and your big floppy sunhat? Or have you got tired of your sparkly sandals and your best hair ribbon?'

'No,' said Alexandra. 'I've got tired of being somebody else all day. Today I'm just going to be me.'

Alexandra's
Plaster
Disaster

Alexandra loved swinging on her garden swing – *wheeeeee*!

Right up over the cherry tree.

Right up over the roof.

Right up to the SKY!

One day Alexandra's mum said, 'You mustn't swing today, Alexandra. It's the rope. It's all ...'

'Shivered?' said Alexandra.

'Eh – no,' said her mum. 'It's all ...'

'Sprunched,' said Alexandra. 'I know, it's shivered and sprunched and ... spiffled!'

'Well anyway,' said her mum, 'don't swing till we get it fixed.'

But Alexandra wanted to swing.

The rope didn't look shivered to her.

It didn't look spiffled or sprunched at all.

But when Alexandra swung way up high, right up to the sky, the rope snapped.

Alexandra flew through the air and landed – thunkety, plunkety, bump – on the grass.

'Owwwwww!' screeched Alexandra. 'My knee is broken.'

'Oh dear,' said Alexandra's mum. 'But it's not broken, Alexandra. It's only a little scratch.'

'There's *blood*!' shrieked Alexandra. 'It's broken!'

'I know,' said Alexandra's mum. 'This is a Plaster Disaster.'

'What's that?' sobbed Alexandra.

'It's when you have an accident and you need a plaster,' said her mum.

'What kind of plaster?' asked Alexandra.

'The Mickey Mouse kind,' said her mum. 'With a kiss inside.'

'A kiss from Mickey Mouse?' asked Alexandra.

'No,' said her mum. 'A kiss from me.'

'Oh,' said Alexandra. 'Will it fix my broken knee?'

'Oh yes,' said her mum.

She put a Mickey Mouse plaster on Alexandra's broken knee, and Alexandra felt much better.

'You shouldn't have swung today, Alexandra,' her mum said later.

'No,' said Alexandra.

'Sorry,' said Alexandra.

'You are a lucky girl,' said Alexandra's mum.

'Lucky?' said Alexandra.

'You could have broken both your knees!' said her mum. 'And we only had one plaster.'

# Alexandra Gets Wet

Alexandra didn't like having her hair washed.

'It makes my eyes prickle,' she said to her mum. 'It hurts if your eyes prickle.'

'Well, you should keep your eyes closed,' said her mum.

'But then I can't *see!*' said Alexandra. 'I don't like that.'

'Let's wait until tomorrow,' said her mum.

The next day Alexandra still didn't like having her hair washed.

'The water goes all in my mouth and I have to swallow it,' she said to her mum. 'It tastes soapy and it slurps in my tummy.'

'Well, you should keep your mouth shut,' said her mum.

'But then I can't *talk*!' said Alexandra. 'Hmm-mmmph-mmmph. I don't like not being able to talk.'

'Let's wait until tomorrow,' said her mum.

The next day Alexandra still didn't like having her hair washed.

'It gets water in my ears,' she said to her mum. 'You can't hear if you have water in your ears. It's all rubbly-wubbly-bubbly.'

'The water comes out in the end,' said her mum. 'Then you can hear again. You just have to wait for it to come out, gurgle-splish!'

'I don't want my ears to gurgle,' said Alexandra.

'Let's wait until tomorrow,' said her mum.

The next day Alexandra still didn't like having her hair washed.

'It makes me ga-ha-asp,' she said to her mum. 'It makes me think I'm going to drown. It's not nice if you drown.'

'You won't drown, Alexandra,' said her mum. 'I'll pick you up and turn you upside down and shake the water out of you so you can breathe again.'

'I don't want you to shake me,' said Alexandra. 'I like standing the right way up.'

'I'll tell you what,' said her mum. 'You can close your eyes, close your mouth and hold your nose, and we'll finish *eversofast*.'

'*Eversofast*,' said Alexandra. 'Promise?'

'I promise,' said her mum.

'OK,' said Alexandra. 'And then I'll be beautiful, won't I?'

'You're always beautiful, Alexandra,' said her mum.

Good Night,
Alexandra

Alexandra didn't like the dark.

'Let's leave your night light on,' said her mum. 'Then it won't be so dark.'

'Yes,' said Alexandra. 'And I think I'd better wear my pink pyjamas. The dark doesn't like pink.'

'Good idea,' said Alexandra's mum, and she helped Alexandra to put on her pink pyjamas.

'It's not very dark,' said her mum. 'I can see your pink pyjamas. Good night, Alexandra.'

'Mu-u-um?' called Alexandra after a while.

'Yes?' said Alexandra's mum, coming into her room.
'What's wrong? Is it the dark again?'

'Yes,' said Alexandra. 'It makes me thirsty.'

'Well, have a little drink of water,' said her mum.

So Alexandra had a little drink, and then her mum said,
'Good night, Alexandra.'

'Mu-u-um?' called Alexandra after a little while.

'Alexandra, it's getting late,' said her mum. 'What's wrong?'

'It's the dark,' said Alexandra. 'It's *whispering*.'

'I've never heard the dark whispering,' said her mum.

'Well, it is,' said Alexandra. 'Listen.'

'I think you're right, Alexandra,' said Alexandra's mum
after a while. 'I can hear whispering. But it's not the dark.
It's just a branch brushing against the window. It's going
*shissh-shooossh, shissh-shooosssh*.'

'Don't!' said Alexandra. 'I can't sleep if something is going
*shissh-shooossh* in the dark. I know! Let's shout, so we can't
hear it.'

'Shooosssh off!' shouted Alexandra's mum.

'Shisssh off!' shouted Alexandra.

But the shisssh-shooossshing sound still shissshed and
shooosshed.

'Tell you what, I'll sing,' said Alexandra's mum, 'so we can't hear it.'

Alexandra closed her eyes, and her mum sang, 'Lavender's blue, dilly-dilly.'

*Shisssh-shooossh*, went the dark.

Then Alexandra's mum sang 'Twinkle, twinkle,' and Alexandra kept her eyes shut.

*Shisssh-shoooosssh*, went the dark.

'Rock-a-bye, baby,' sang Alexandra's mum.

*Shisssh-shooossh*, went the dark softly.

But Alexandra didn't hear it.

Because Alexandra ... was ... fast ... asleep.

Good night, Alexandra.

**Alexandra** loves swinging and splashing and her bright red shoes. And her mum. She doesn't much like having her hair washed, though, and she definitely does not like the dark.

These warm stories of the everyday life of a small girl by Ireland's first Children's Laureate, originally broadcast on RTÉ's *The Den*, are great for reading aloud.

Little Island www.littleisland.ie

ISBN: 978-1-908195-87-6

9 781908 195876

Published in DUBLIN UNESCO City of Literature

£6.99
UK only